Sanne te Loo
This is Yours

Lemniscaat

Of all things imaginable,
I like drawing the most.
But a sheet of paper was
much too small for me.

First published in the UK in 2019 by Lemniscaat Ltd, Kemp House, 152 City Road, London EC1V 2NX
Distributed worldwide by Thames & Hudson, 181A High Holborn, London WC1V 7QX

ISBN 13: 978-1-78807-043-0 (Hardcover)
Printing and binding: Wilco bv, Amersfoort, The Netherlands

First UK edition

www.lemniscaat.co.uk

And in the streets, people would walk all over my drawings.

I finally found some space.
But when my drawing was almost finished,
it started to rain.

An old man came out.
'I'm Anselmo,' he said. 'I'm a painter, just like you.
Do you want to come in to take shelter?'

I had never seen anything like this!
Anselmo said cheerfully,
'What a mess, huh?'

He didn't seem to care about the chaos.
'Look at that spot, it's like a panther! Or a camel!'
I looked through my eyelashes, just like he did,
and I saw a small spider, a jellyfish and a flamingo.

With Anselmo I found space.
And the rain didn't wash away
my drawings anymore.
As often as I could, I would
be with him.

'This is what I'm working on,'
Anselmo said.
'It isn't finished by far –
do you want to help me?'

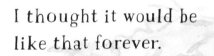

I thought it would be
like that forever.

But one day, Anselmo told me that he was
too old to continue living on his own.
He would return to the place where he came from.
'Parrot island?' I asked.
Anselmo nodded.

Anselmo was really gone.
His house now belonged to a posh lady.
'At last, there you are!' she cried when she saw me.
'You are Anselmo's boy. He has been thinking about you.'
And she beckoned me inside.

The room was exactly as before.
But against the wall sat a large blank canvas.
'Everything changes,' the lady said.
'But this will stay the same.
This is yours.'